Hi there,

I'm David Warner, Australian cricketer,
and I'm really excited to introduce you to
my new series of kids' books called
The Kaboom Kid.

Little Davey Warner is 'the Kaboom Kid',
a cricket-mad eleven-year-old who wants to
play cricket with his mates every minute of
the day, just like I did as a kid.

Davey gets into all sorts of scrapes with his
friends, but mainly he has a great time playing
cricket for his cricket club, the Sandhill Sluggers,
and helping them win lots of matches.

If you're into cricket, and I know you are, then you
will love these books. Enjoy *The Kaboom Kid.*

David Warner

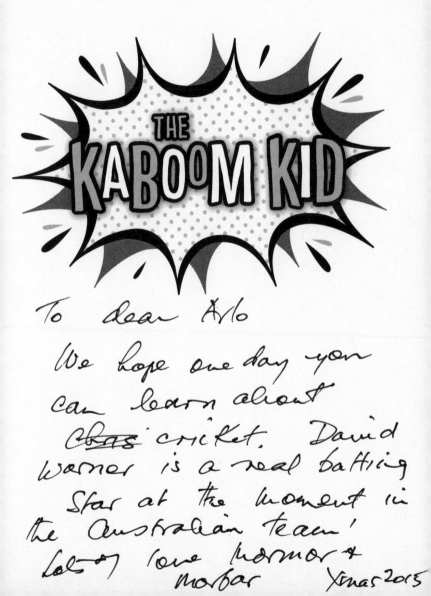

THE KABOOM KID

To dear Arlo

We hope one day you
can learn about
~~class~~ cricket. David
Warner is a real batting
star at the moment in
the Australian team!
Lots of love marmor &
marpar   Xmas 2015

THE KABOOM KID

The Big Switch

DAVID WARNER

with J. V. McGEE, Illustrated by JULES FABER

SIMON & SCHUSTER
AUSTRALIA
A CBS COMPANY

THE KABOOM KID – THE BIG SWITCH
First published in Australia in 2014 by
Simon & Schuster (Australia) Pty Limited
Suite 19A, Level 1, 450 Miller Street, Cammeray, NSW 2062

10 9 8 7 6 5 4

A CBS Company
Sydney New York London Toronto New Delhi
Visit our website at www.simonandschuster.com.au

National Library of Australia Cataloguing-in-Publication entry
Author: Warner, David Andrew, author.
Title: The kaboom kid: the big switch/
                 David Warner and J.V. McGee.
ISBN: 9781925030785 (paperback)
                 9781925030792 (ebook)
Target Audience: Upper primary school students.
Subjects: Warner, David Andrew.
                 Cricket – Australia – Juvenile literature.
                 Cricket players – Australia – Juvenile literature.
                 Cricket – Batting – Juvenile literature.
Other Authors: McGee, J. V., author.
Dewey Number: 796.3580994

Cover design by Hannah Janzen
Cover and internal illustrations by Jules Faber
Inside cover photograph of adult David Warner © Quinn Rooney/Getty Images
Typeset by Midland Typesetters, Australia
Printed and bound in Australia by Griffin Press

FSC
www.fsc.org
MIX
Paper from
responsible sources
FSC® C009448

The paper this book is printed on is certified
against the Forest Stewardship Council® Standards.
Griffin Press holds FSC chain of custody certification
SGS-COC-005088. FSC promotes environmentally
responsible, socially beneficial and economically
viable management of the world's forests.

FOR MUM & DAD

CONTENTS

CHAPTER 1

KABOOM TAKES A BOW

Davey Warner gripped his bat. Squinting in the sunlight, he watched as his arch-rival, Josh Jarrett, paced out his run-up at the far wicket. At last Josh turned and faced him. Even from this distance, Davey could see the determination in Josh's eyes as the star all-rounder gave the ball a final polish.

This was it. The last ball of the match, and Josh's team, Shimmer Bay, were ahead by five runs. Davey's team, the Sandhill Sluggers, had put up a fight, but they'd been the underdogs from the start. Now Shimmer Bay appeared certain to win the match and seize the number-one spot on the ladder.

Davey glanced around. Josh, who was Shimmer Bay's captain, had changed his field because Davey was a left-hander. Josh's team played like real professionals.

'Come on, Josh, bowl him a bouncer!' someone shouted from the sideline. The Shimmer Bay supporters were as determined as their players to see the Sluggers go down. They were always shouting out advice that even Josh Jarrett ignored, despite the fact everyone said he was cricket's most well-mannered, best-behaved all-round Mr Perfect.

Davey glanced over at the Sluggers'
supporters and players. Benny, their coach,
was present, but he was deep in conversation,
and Davey guessed he *wasn't* talking about
cricket. Davey's best mate, Sunil, gave him
a wave. There was his friend George, and
Kevin, who'd skipped Vietnamese school to
catch the game. Even his big brother, Steve,
had turned up.

'Go, Davey! You can do it!' Davey's mum
and dad were cheering from the sideline,
but they didn't sound confident. Why
would they? The Sluggers were as good as
finished.

Davey took his position at the crease.
Trying to focus his mind, he tapped his bat
on the ground. It was his special bat made
of English willow and signed by his heroes,
Ricky Ponting and Shane Warne. The bat was
called Kaboom, and it felt heavy and powerful

in his hands. He raised Kaboom to his lips and gave it a kiss for good luck. He was ready.

Josh began his run-up. He pounded towards the bowler's crease and let the ball fly. It was fast and short down the leg side.

Davey swung Kaboom and hit the ball clean and true. It soared into the sky and away, over the trees by the boundary. Six! *Six!*

Davey Warner had snatched the match from the jaws of defeat! The Sandhill Sluggers had won!

The Sluggers and their supporters cheered wildly. The Shimmer Bay supporters were already packing up.

Davey looked down at Kaboom. 'Thanks, mate,' he said to his special bat. 'I couldn't have done it without you.'

Kaboom nodded before leaping out of Davey's hands. The bat waddled out into the middle of the pitch . . . and took a bow . . .

Davey heard a squawk. The fielders had turned into seagulls and were flying off in every direction. Even Josh Jarrett had sprouted a pair of wings.

The other batter ran towards him. It was Max, his dog – and he was wearing a tutu in the Sluggers' colours of green and gold.

Max gave him a big wet kiss on the face. Ugh! Max smelt bad – he must have rolled in something.

Oh no! It's a dream! Davey woke with a start. Max was standing on top of him, licking his face. The dog stank like something dead.

'Get off!' Davey shouted. He pushed Max onto the floor and squinted in the morning sunshine. He couldn't believe it. It had all seemed so real. Josh Jarrett, the Shimmer Bay supporters, Mum and Dad looking unsure . . . Kaboom taking a bow – and Max in a tutu. No, it definitely had been a dream.

And then reality hit, and Davey felt like pulling the blanket over his head and going back to sleep until the cricket season was over. Because the truth was, just three days earlier the Sandhill Sluggers had *lost* to Shimmer Bay. Davey hadn't hit a six – instead, all-round Mr Perfect Josh Jarrett had. And worse, Shimmer Bay were now top of the ladder, leaving the Sluggers stuck at equal second with the Crabby Creek Crickets.

It was too terrible to contemplate. Davey pulled the blanket over his head and tried to think about something else. Then he remembered it was the summer holidays and he and Sunil could meet up with the others for a game of cricket on the beach. Life wasn't so bad after all.

He threw the blanket off.

Davey's mum stuck her head around the door. 'Ah, you're awake. Better get up. Can't be late for your first day back at school!'

Davey pulled the blanket back up over his head and let out a groan.

'Good heavens!' he heard his mum exclaim. 'What have you been rolling in, you dreadful dog?'

Max barked. At least someone was happy the school year had started.

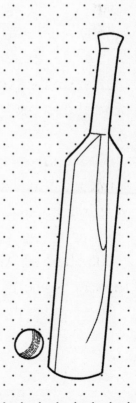

CHAPTER 2
MID-OFF MAX

Mrs Trundle, the school principal, had made it clear on countless occasions that Max was not to attend school under any circumstances whatsoever.

Unfortunately, Max had never paid any attention. So when Davey took off on his bike

in the direction of Sandhill Flats Primary, the dog was close behind, nipping the bike's back wheel and yapping loudly.

Davey found his friends already playing cricket at the bottom of C playground. No teacher was in sight, so Max was in the clear.

Sunil screwed up his face. 'What's that smell?! Warner! Have you been rolling in doggy doo again?' He laughed.

'Deep, you'll be in it in a minute,' Davey replied, pushing his friend so hard he almost fell into a puddle of what looked suspiciously like runny poo. 'It's Max,' he said.

Kevin McNab and George Pepi wandered over, holding their noses. 'Good to see you, Warner,' Kevin said in a nasally voice. He put his arm around Davey's shoulders. 'Come to learn how to play cricket, have you?'

'Very funny, McNab,' Davey said.

'I heard what happened against Shimmer Bay. You Sluggers obviously need help.'

'And you need a brain transplant.'

It wasn't exactly a killer line, but Kevin seemed to like it because he grinned. 'Oh well, give me a call if you need any tips. Maybe one day I'll join the team.'

Davey wished Kevin *would* join the Sluggers, but he couldn't because his mum made him go to Vietnamese school on Saturdays, which was when the Sluggers played.

'Come on, guys. It's nearly bell time!' Sunil called.

When everyone was in position, George bowled a leg break to Kevin, who lofted it towards the mid-off fence. Max caught it on the full. Kevin was out.

'Stinking dog!' Kevin threw down his bat. 'You're in, Warner. But watch out for that dishlicker. He's getting good!'

Davey took Kaboom out of his backpack, then pulled out his special cricket cap and put it on his head. It was just a faded green trucker's hat, but Davey called it his 'baggy green' and had stuck a picture of the Australian cricket team's badge on the front.

'Okay, Deep, give me all you've got!' he shouted.

Sunil bowled a fast one outside Davey's off stump.

Davey drove it straight into Max's open jaws. Max smiled through his catch.

Davey was out for a duck. 'Max, you're a menace!'

Sunil guffawed. 'He's good is what he is. But, hey, can't get out first ball. Go again.'

Davey hated being given a second chance almost as much as he hated getting out. He faced up again.

Once more Max caught him out. The dog now had a hat-trick of catches.

'You'll have to do better than that if you want to beat Max the Axe,' Kevin called out.

Davey glared at his dog. 'Max the Muppet, more likely.'

Max grinned the way dogs do.

'Hey, Shorty! Out again? Maybe you should give up and play a *real* game.' Big Mo Clouter, the school's best footy player, had appeared out of nowhere and was standing menacingly beside the wicket while Sunil prepared to bowl.

Six years of putting up with Mo had taught Davey that the best thing to do was pretend the swaggering lump of wood was invisible.

Sunil did the same. 'One more chance!' he called to Davey before running in. But as he was about to bowl the ball, Mo stuck his foot out and tripped him.

It was a pathetic trick and Davey could hardly believe it had worked, but now Sunil was sprawled on the ground eating dirt.

Mo hooted then gagged. 'Aww, that dog's stinky! I gotta get out of here! Weird smells make me sick!' He ran off in the direction of the toilets.

Sunil got to his feet and dusted himself off. He turned to run in again.

'Warrr-*ner*!'

Now Davey remembered why the summer holidays had been so sweet (if he didn't count the loss to Shimmer Bay). Sure, there had been lots of cricket, going to the beach, barbecues for dinner, Christmas presents (a set of wickets and a brand new ball), a fair bit of screen time . . . But what had made the holidays so perfect was that Davey hadn't heard of nor seen Mr Mudge, or 'Smudge', as he and his friends sometimes called him. Not once. Now here was the grumpiest, most tired, most *unfair* of school teachers in all of Sandhill Flats, and he was clearly unimpressed to be back at school after six weeks doing whatever Mudges do.

'Yes, Mr Mudge?'

'What is that dog doing at school? *AGAIN!*
How many times have you been told?' Mr
Mudge marched up to Max and grabbed him
by the collar. 'Aargh! What's that smell?!'

Max sat down hard in the dirt, a look
of profound disappointment on his face.
He wasn't going anywhere.

'Get this malodorous mutt out of here
THIS MINUTE!' Mr Mudge bawled.

Even from a distance, Davey could see
that the teacher's ears, which stuck out from
under lank grey hair, were turning crimson.
Obviously Mudge was even sorrier than Davey
that the holidays were over.

'Yes, Mr Mudge,' Davey said meekly. 'Max,
home!' he commanded.

Max looked balefully at Davey and stayed put.

'Max, HOME! NOW!'

Max didn't move a whisker.

Davey trudged over, grabbed his dog by the collar and dragged him towards the school's side gate. 'Straight home,' he said into the animal's ear, before giving him a quick pat and pushing him through. 'No side trips.'

Max threw him a look that said *I can't promise anything* and slunk off.

When Davey returned to his friends, Mr Mudge was lecturing the boys on school rules about dogs and cricket.

'I'll be watching you lot,' he said. 'Do anything silly and I'll be putting an end to all

this cricket.' He looked at Davey. 'And get rid of that hat! You're out of uniform!'

Finally Mr Mudge finished his tirade and turned to leave.

'A few more balls, Deep,' Davey said quietly to Sunil.

At that moment the bell rang.

'Put it away *immediately*!' Mr Mudge bellowed as he stomped off.

The boys gathered their belongings and trudged in the direction of the quadrangle.

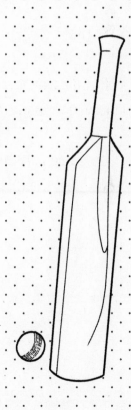

CHAPTER 3

MO'S MAMBO

'I need performers and volunteers to help with this year's Welcome to Kindy showcase. All you clever year sixes in particular – this is your chance to shine!' The smiling teacher addressing the assembly was new at the school.

She'll stop smiling pretty soon, once things settle down, thought Davey, who was sitting up the back with the rest of Year Six.

It was the first assembly of the year, and it seemed to be dragging on forever. There'd been announcements about no ball games in B playground and no running in A playground, and now the Welcome to Kindy showcase. No wonder everyone was whispering and fidgeting and scratching.

The new teacher pressed on. 'So come and talk to me about—'

Suddenly Mrs Trundle burst into rhythmic clapping. The whole school clapped back.

When everyone was quiet, Mrs Trundle seized the microphone. 'Thank you, Ms Maro,' she said, nodding in the direction of the now startled new teacher.

But Ms Maro wouldn't be silenced. 'Students, come and talk to me about your ideas for the showcase,' she shouted. 'Singing, dancing – anything you think the kindies and their parents will enjoy.' She looked across at Mrs Trundle and smiled. 'Thank you, Mrs Trundle. I've finished now.'

Mrs Trundle's eye twitched. She waved a wad of papers at the students. 'It's time to join your new classes,' she said in an imperious voice. 'Listen for your name, remember your teacher and, at the end of assembly, follow that teacher to your new classroom.'

Davey and his friends looked at each other. There were usually three Year Six classes, so chances were they'd be split up.

'We'll start with Year One,' Mrs Trundle said, looking across at Year Six with a smirk on her face.

Year Six groaned and zoned out.

Around four hours later, Davey came to.

'David Warner . . .' Mrs Trundle's voice was sounding tired. 'Sunil Deep . . .'

'Yes!' Davey whispered.

'Mo Clouter . . .'

Davey sucked in a breath.

'George Pepi . . .' Mrs Trundle's voice sounded husky. 'Bella Ferosi . . . and Kevin McNab.'

The boys punched the air. They were all in the same class. It was going to be one awesome year.

'Your class is 6M, and your teacher is . . .'

Davey and his friends stared at each other in horror. The M in 6M could stand for only one thing.

Mrs Trundle's voice was almost gone. '. . . Mr Mudge,' she wheezed.

'Warner, Deep, McNab and Pepi are to sit at different tables. There'll be no talking about cricket in my class!'

It was still morning on the first day of the school year and Mr Mudge's ears were already vermilion. 'Warner, you sit there.' Mudge pointed to the place between Bella Ferosi and Mo Clouter. 'Hopefully Bella and Mo can keep you on track.'

Bella, who was school captain and had never answered a question incorrectly since she was born, gave her neat brown ponytail a flick. She smiled kindly at Davey as he trudged towards her.

Davey pulled out his chair, set down his belongings and squeezed in next to Mo.

Mo made a face and grabbed Davey's ruler. 'I'll show you how to play cricket, Shorty,' he said, brandishing the ruler like a cutlass.

Davey smiled bitterly before looking around for his friends, now scattered to the far corners of the room. Sunil made a sympathetic face. There was nothing to be done, so Davey tried to tune in to the drone of Mr Mudge's voice.

'For my holiday, I went on a lawn bowls tour up the coast,' Mudge was saying. 'Every day we played in a new place against a new team. It was a dream come true!' He threw his arms wide in excitement.

Davey had never heard the old grump speak with such passion.

'So now, I'd like *you* to write a short recount about something you did during the holidays.' Mudge smiled. 'There's just one rule.' He raised his finger and pointed at Davey, Sunil, George and Kevin in turn. 'No cricket. If I read anything about cricket, you'll be picking up papers all lunchtime.'

Back in third grade, Davey had worked out that Mudge didn't like cricket much. Now it struck him – Mudge *despised* cricket.

Davey looked at the blank piece of paper in front of him. What else was there to write about? Uncle Vernon's record-breaking burp at Christmas lunch? The day Dad fell off the veranda and landed on Mum's cactus? Or when Sunil nearly choked on a Whopper

Chomp lolly, and Davey had to thrash him on the back to save him? All fun times, but not as much fun as playing cricket.

Suddenly he felt something sharp on his cheek. He looked up. Mo was laughing silently. A dozen or so paper spitballs were lined up on the desk in front of him. Wielding Davey's ruler like a tennis racquet, Mo was batting spitballs in his neighbour's direction.

Next Mo took aim at Bella. The school captain, who'd had her head down all the while, was studiously writing, her free hand covering her work so no one could copy.

Davey peeled the spitball off his cheek and tried to focus again on his story.

'*Ouch!*'

Davey looked up. Now Mo had his head down and was working quietly. The ruler lay by Davey's hand.

Bella picked a spitball off her face and raised her hand. 'Mr Mudge,' she said in a clear voice.

'Yes, Bella?'

'Davey Warner is hitting spitballs with his ruler. One got me in the face.'

Mo sniggered.

Mr Mudge's ears turned beetroot. 'Whhh–a–a–a–t? Warner, I'm giving you your first warning. One more and you're on lunchtime detention. Hand me that ruler. Now get back to work!'

Davey passed the ruler to Mudge. There was no point trying to clear his name. Instead, he tried to get on with his schoolwork.

But as he scribbled out the story of his dad's cactus accident, his mind returned to Mo's trick. He had to admit that Mo was on to something. He'd been hitting left and right, switching the ruler back and forth as if he was playing tennis.

Maybe, Davey thought, he could try a switch like that when he was batting. And maybe, then, he could beat Max at his own game . . .

CHAPTER 4

TRAINING TRY-OUT

'Out!' Sunil held up his index finger.

George punched the air. 'Mouldy Max strikes again!'

Max had caught Davey out at silly mid-off for the hundredth time that day.

Davey threw down Kaboom and ran at his dog, hooting. Max took off, tearing across Flatter Park towards the beach.

After a minute or so, Davey stopped, puffed. He looked back to where the Sluggers were still training. Benny, the coach, was lugging cricket gear across the park.

'Max!' Davey called. 'Back here now!' For once, Max obeyed and together they trotted back.

'Hey, guys! Sorry I'm late! Had to see a man about a dog.' Benny dumped the gear on the grass. He bent over to catch his breath, clutching his bulging tummy as if it might explode.

Benny was almost always late for training – and matches, too, sometimes. The team didn't mind. Someone would bring a ball, some bats, a set of wickets or two, and they'd just get on with it.

Now Benny straightened up. 'Gather round, guys,' he called. 'We need to debrief.'

When everyone was standing in a ragged circle, Benny launched into his 'pep' talk.

'It's a real shame we lost to Shimmer Bay,' he said. 'Fact is, they probably deserve to be top dogs. That Josh Jarrett, in particular, is real class.'

Davey and Sunil looked at each other and rolled their eyes. Josh Jarrett might be 'real class' but he was also a pain in the posterior.

'Anyway, no use crying over spilt milk. Next match is against Batfish Beach Bantams. They're not much chop, but it's going to be tough.'

Davey, George and Sunil tried not to laugh. Benny always feared the worst. Weirdly, the more pessimistic Benny was, the better the Sluggers played.

'And as for the game after next, against the Crabby Creek Crickets . . .' Benny shook his head. 'They're equal number two with us now and looking good, so I can't see how we'll win that one.' He smiled sadly. 'Never mind. You Sluggers keep plugging on. Who knows? A bit of luck might come our way . . .' He scratched his tummy and let out a loud burp. 'So, back to what you were doing, while I go and grab myself a snack from the shop. Been so busy today I didn't have a proper lunch.'

Davey knew that Benny was never busy. He ran the corner shop with his wife, Barb, but she seemed to do most of the work. Benny read the paper a lot and was always popping out.

As Benny turned to leave, he screwed up his nose. 'What's that smell?' he said.

Max barked and took off after a seagull.

The Sluggers went back to their positions. They didn't mind that Benny had nicked off. It meant they could play cricket without an adult telling them what to do.

Davey was fielding on the boundary. It gave him time to think. Mo Clouter's pesky face appeared in his mind's eye, and he recalled how the great lug had swung the ruler like a tennis racquet. Mo had called it cricket. *Yeah, sure.* But thinking on it some more, Davey wondered whether he could try it not only to outsmart Max the Mutt but to help defeat the Bantams on Saturday.

'You're in again, Warner!' Sunil was waving to him.

Davey collected Kaboom from the sideline and took his place at the crease. He glared at Max, who was still fielding at silly mid-off. The way things were going, soon Max would be playing for Australia and have his own baggy green.

'Watch this,' he growled at his dog.

George bowled a leg break. Davey turned quickly, swapped the position of his hands and tried to drive it right-handed past Ivy Mundine. He missed, and the ball flew through to Dylan, the keeper.

A few balls later, Davey tried the trick again. This time he got an edge to the ball, which almost went onto the wicket.

Max barked as if to say, *Give up, boss. You know it's useless.*

'Stop mucking about, Warner!' George shouted from the other end of the pitch. 'Hit it!'

Davey considered his options. He could try the trick one more time or forget it as a bad idea. He decided to give it one more try.

George came in to bowl. Again it was a leg break. Davey turned, swapped his hands and bam! He hit the ball straight over the boundary and into the swamp.

'That good enough for you?' he called to George.

George nodded slowly, and gave the thumbs-up. 'Not bad, Warner.' He pointed. 'You might want to get Max, though.'

Davey saw Max leap into the swamp and lope through the mucky water in search of the ball. The dog ducked and dived before dashing out and back across the park, trailing slime. At least he had the ball in his mouth.

'Now that dog is totally pongo!' Sunil said, as Max shook slime all over them.

Davey looked smug. 'Maybe, but he didn't catch me!'

'And he's given me an idea,' Sunil said, a malevolent grin on his face.

Davey raised an eyebrow. 'Yeah? What?'

Sunil tapped the side of his nose. 'You'll see.'

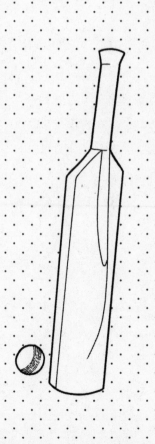

CHAPTER 5

TRICK OR TREAT

That night, Davey's mum made him wash Max.
It was the last thing he felt like doing, but even
he had to admit that it was either that or send
Max to the dog pound.

Sunil and his little sister, Lata, who lived
next door, came over to help. They held Max

by the collar while Davey ran the hose over him before squirting some doggy shampoo onto his back.

'Can I help?' Lata asked. She wasn't much taller than Max, but she managed to rub the shampoo into Max's fur and work up a lather. Now the dog looked like a walking bubble bath.

'It's a pity, really,' Sunil said, sucking noisily on a Whopper Chomp, his favourite lolly. 'Max has been an inspiration.' He pulled the lolly packet out of his pocket and offered it to Davey and Lata. 'Here, let's finish these.'

Davey took a lolly before Sunil could change his mind. 'What do you mean "an inspiration"?' he said.

'You'll find out,' Sunil said. 'It'll be brilliant. Mo's gonna flip.' He grabbed Lata by the hand. 'Come on, you. We've got work to do,' he said,

before heading down the side path. 'See you tomorrow.'

Davey shook his head. He guessed Sunil was off to play with his chemistry set. But why?

Davey turned on the tap again and began to hose Max, but the dog ran off. By the time Davey caught him and finished towelling him down, it was dark. Now Max smelt like a mix of Hubba Bubba and hospital.

Davey couldn't get to sleep that night. For one thing, Max was snoring on the floor. For another, the dog's unique odour filled the room. As Davey breathed it in, his thoughts turned to his tricky switch-hit idea. It wasn't an easy shot, but he'd managed to pull it off once at training.

Maybe, with lots of practice, he could do it whenever he wanted. It could become his secret weapon, something he could use not only to outsmart Max, but to help the Sluggers outdo the Batfish Beach Bantams and even the Crabby Creek Crickets. Maybe (and this was a BIG maybe), one day he could use his secret weapon to hit Josh Jarrett out of the park for real and help take down Shimmer Bay Juniors.

But to get it right, he'd have to practise it every morning, every lunchtime and every afternoon. There was no other way.

Just before he finally fell asleep, Davey remembered Sunil. *I wonder what he's up to? And what's that smell?*

Cricket before school now followed a pattern. Max would catch Davey, then George, then Kevin – and George would bowl Sunil.

This time, when it was Davey's turn to bat, he decided to try his switch hit. He missed and nearly fell onto the stumps. The second time he tried it, Kevin almost caught him behind the wicket. The third time, it kind of worked, but the ball didn't go far. But the fourth time, it worked like a dream – and almost took out the eye of Mr Mudge, who had just appeared around the corner of the toilet block.

'Oh-oh,' George said. 'Smudge not happy.'

Spotting the approaching teacher, Max had the sense to make a beeline for the side gate. By the time Mr Mudge reached them, the dog was halfway home.

'Watch where you hit that ball or I'll be confiscating it.' Mr Mudge was out of breath and puffing like a steam train.

'And don't think I didn't see that dog, Warner,' he said. 'This is your last warning. If he's here again, you're going straight to Mrs Trundle.'

'Yes, Sir,' Davey said.

Sunil gulped, swallowing the lolly he'd been sucking. 'Mr Mudge?'

'Yes, Sunil?'

'Could I go into class early today? I want to practise my twelve times table.'

'Of course, Sunil,' Mr Mudge said, looking pleased. 'I wish some of these other ninnies,' he pointed at Davey, 'would spend more time on their schoolwork and less time playing cricket.'

Sunil smiled sweetly so his dimple showed. 'Thanks, Mr Mudge.' He picked up his bag and headed towards the classrooms. 'See you there,' he called.

When Davey and the others went into class, Sunil was already at his desk, his maths book open in front of him.

'How'd you go, Deep?' Davey said. 'Learn anything?'

'Twelve times twelve equals 147.' Sunil smiled and winked at his friends.

Mr Mudge appeared in the doorway. 'Ah, Sunil, how pleasing it is to see a student put in some effort. You won't regret it.'

'I find maths so much more interesting than cricket, Mr Mudge,' Sunil said.

'And it'll take you a lot further in life, young man.' Mr Mudge surveyed the room. 'Mr Deep here has been studying in his own time,' he said, 'setting an excellent example for the rest of you.'

'Sir?' Bella had her hand up. 'I study in my own time every morning before school, during lunch and after school. It's *one* reason why I mostly come first in things.' She gave her ponytail a flick.

'Thank you, Bella.' Mr Mudge's ears were candyfloss pink. 'You, too, set an excellent example for some of your less conscientious classmates.' He glared at George, then at Kevin, and then Davey.

His ears still rosy, Mr Mudge moved on. 'Speaking of setting an example, I want all the class to get involved in the Welcome to Kindy showcase. Ms Maro is open to any ideas.'

He made an odd face that Davey presumed was a smile. 'It's such a lovely way to introduce our newest pupils and their families to Sandhill Flats Primary. I'm sure some of you remember when you were in kindy and attended the showcase.'

'Arrgaaahhhggrrreeeeuuuwww!' The awful sound was loud in Davey's ear.

It was Mo. He appeared to be having some kind of fit. In front of him lay an open packet of Whopper Chomps.

Davey glanced back at Mr Mudge. The teacher's ears had turned carnation red.

'Clouter! Have you been eating lollies in class?'

Mo shook his head but was unable to speak. 'Arrgggrreeeuwwwahhhhh!' was all he could manage.

'What is the matter, young man?' Mr Mudge appeared perplexed.

Finally Mo got a word out. 'The smell! The smell!' He pointed to the bag of lollies. 'There – there's something in there!'

Davey became aware of a horrible stink. It was a bit like runny poached eggs and a bit like Max's farts after he stole the Christmas pudding.

Obviously Bella had caught a whiff of it too. 'It's disgusssting!' she screamed.

Davey glanced over at Sunil. His friend was engrossed in his times tables again.

'Get those lollies out of the room this minute!' Mudge's ears had turned violet. 'Clouter, you're on detention!'

CHAPTER 6

SWITCH GLITCH

Mr Mudge soon deduced that while Mo Clouter may have been breaking class rules by trying to sneak a lolly, he wasn't responsible for the awful aroma emanating from the Whopper Chomp packet. Who *was* responsible, well, Mr Mudge couldn't be sure, because no one would confess to the crime.

Mo said he didn't know where the packet had come from. 'It was on my desk when I came in,' he whined. 'Whopper Chomps are my *favourite*.'

Davey tried to appear as confused as everyone else. But when Mr Mudge discovered that the Whopper Chomp packet contained a small open vial of rotten egg gas, Davey's suspicions were confirmed. Sunil's chemistry set was to blame. Mo must have come to the same conclusion, because he glared at Sunil with pure loathing.

Deeply unimpressed by the prank, Mr Mudge put the entire class on lunchtime detention for two weeks. 'Don't think you'll be sitting around, either,' Mudge barked. 'I have plenty of jobs for you.'

Everyone groaned, except Bella. Davey was particularly despondent. He needed those lunchtimes to practise his new switch hit before the weekend. Now he only had mornings and afternoons to get it right.

At recess, Sunil tried to console him. 'At least I didn't waste any Whopper Chomps on Mo,' he said. 'Here.' He pulled a sweet from his pocket and handed it to Davey. 'There's more where that came from.'

The vampire teeth lolly was coated in sand and fluff. Davey gave it a quick dust and popped it in his mouth.

Sunil turned to his friends. 'You gotta admit it was a good trick.'

Kevin and George nodded, impressed. 'How'd you do it?' Kevin asked.

'Iron filings and vinegar. Easy.'

Davey sucked thoughtfully on his Whopper Chomp. 'Deep, you're a master. Now we just have to work out how to get out of lunchtime detention.'

By the time the weekend came around, Davey and the rest of 6M had wasted hours of good cricket time picking up papers, sorting last year's lost property, and cleaning out Mrs Trundle's storeroom.

Davey had tried his best to practise his switch hit before and after school but, even though he was improving, he doubted it would be enough.

The match against the Batfish Beach Bantams was to be played at the Bantams' home ground, which gave them an edge, according to Benny. Still, the Sluggers had a few supporters, including Max, Davey's mum and dad, and Sunil's dad and his little sister, Lata, who was a fan and didn't like to miss a match.

When Sunil won the toss, he elected to bat first. 'Warner, Pepi, you're in,' he called. 'Now get out there and hit those Bantams for six.'

'Yeah!' Lata called from the sideline. 'Do it, Davey!'

Davey put on his helmet and adjusted his pads. With Kaboom in his hands, he felt ready for anything. There was no way the Bantams were going to outdo the Sluggers today, he decided.

After pulling on his gloves, he followed George onto the pitch, and took his position at the crease. When everyone was ready, the umpire gave the nod.

The first ball was a bouncer, and Davey let it go through to the keeper. He hadn't forgotten Benny's advice to take his time.

The second ball was wide.

It wasn't until the fifth ball that Davey swung Kaboom, but he only got an edge to it and was almost caught behind.

'Come on, Warner!' Sunil was shouting from the boundary line. 'Where's your secret weapon?'

Max barked. *Yeah, where is it, boss?* he seemed to say.

Davey wiggled his shoulders to relax, then took his position.

The bowler eyed him from the other end, before turning to go back to his mark. Then he ran in and let the ball fly.

It was heading down the leg side. Now was his chance. He turned, switched hands and swung his bat. He felt the ball graze the edge.

'Howzat?' The Bantams were jumping up and down like battery bunnies.

Davey looked towards the bowler's end. The umpire raised his index finger in the air.

'Out!' he called.

'Out!' the bowler called.

'Ouch', you mean, Davey thought as he walked back to the boundary. Not only was he out, he was out for a duck.

After that, the Sluggers faltered then collapsed. George was caught at square leg for fifteen. Ivy started well and managed a four before being run out for eleven.

Then the middle order crumbled, and the Sluggers were all out for fifty-seven.

At morning tea, Benny was gloomy. 'They've done well,' he said, scratching his tummy anxiously. 'It's going to be tough from here on.' He looked at Davey. 'Remember what I said? No silly moves or tricky business. So what were you up to today?'

'Dunno,' Davey mumbled, giving the grass a good kick.

Sunil slapped him on the back. 'Don't worry, Warner. Leave it to us bowlers. We'll go in hard.'

Benny jingled his car keys in his pocket. 'I've got to nick off for a short while,' he said, surveying the circle of faces. 'No dreaming out on the field, okay? Everyone on the ball.'

Sunil hadn't been joking. He seemed determined to turn the match around, and had most of the team stand in close in an attacking field.

It worked, and the first Bantam was caught in slips for five runs. The other opener didn't last much longer, out for nine, caught at square leg by Ivy.

But following a middle-order slump, the Bantams' tail wagged, scoring plenty of quick runs to bring them almost level. With four balls to go, they were only three behind.

George bowled one down the leg side. The Bantam batter hooked it high.

'Mine!' Davey shouted, running to get under the ball. He caught it – but he fumbled and the ball tumbled to the ground.

'Aaaarggh!' The Bantams had scored two more. Now they needed just two runs off two balls to win.

George showed no sign of nerves as he prepared to bowl. His first delivery was a leg break. The batter tried to get to it, but misjudged the line and the ball went through to Dylan.

There was one ball to go. George bowled a flipper. This time the batter misjudged the length. The ball struck the wicket with a *thunk*, sending the bails flying.

'Out!'

The umpire raised his index finger.

Phew, Davey thought.

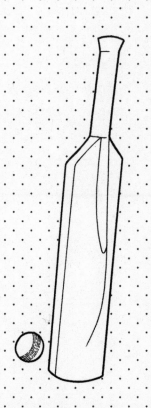

CHAPTER 7

PRACTICE
IMPOSSIBLE

Before going to sleep that night, Davey had
a chat with Ricky Ponting. He often talked
to Ricky, whose face stared out from a
dog-eared poster that was stuck to the wall
behind his bed. Someone (Sunil) had climbed
up and drawn a pointy beard on Ricky's chin
and coloured in two teeth. But while the

poster was fading, the Test cricketer's smile never did.

Davey was still smarting from his duck that morning, not to mention the dropped catch. If it hadn't been for George, who'd kept his cool under pressure, the Sluggers would have lost the match and possibly their equal second place on the ladder.

Now, as Davey lay in bed, he turned his head on a funny angle and looked up to Ricky for advice. *Should I give up on my secret weapon?* He stared hard at the face above him, so hard that his eyes began to water and he couldn't focus. Suddenly there was a flicker, and Davey could have sworn he saw his hero wink. Or was it a trick of the light?

''Night.' His mum was at the door. 'Someone wants to come in.'

Max leapt onto the bed and licked Davey all over his face. It was disgusting.

'Get off!' Davey gave the dog a push.

'Everyone drops catches occasionally,' his mum said, reading his mind. 'And even though it didn't work today, I reckon you'll get that switch hit thing working, with a bit more practice.'

She bent down and gave him a kiss that was much nicer than Max's.

'Now, I meant to tell you,' she said, ruffling his hair. 'I've volunteered for us to help out at Uncle Vernon's nursing home after school for the next week or so. We'll give all the old people a cup of tea and have a chat with them. Nothing too hard, and it makes such a difference to their day.'

'But—'

'You'll still have plenty of time to play cricket before school and at lunchtime, won't you?'

'Yeahhh,' Davey said, with his fingers crossed.

His mum gave him another kiss. 'So, off to sleep,' she said, switching off the bedside lamp. At the door she stopped. 'What does Ricky think about your secret weapon?'

'He reckons I should keep at it.'

'See?' she said. 'Practice makes perfect.'

Davey's secret weapon may have been looking pretty ordinary, but Sandhill Flats Primary had never looked so good. Thanks to the efforts of 6M while on lunchtime detention, the playground, storerooms, hall and library had all been tidied, cleaned, sorted and organised. Bella Ferosi had quickly taken charge, displaying quite a talent for giving orders.

Some students worked hard. Davey Warner, Sunil Deep, George Pepi and Kevin McNab were not among them. It was only when Mr Mudge asked for volunteers to weed and water the petunias outside Mrs Trundle's office that the boys showed any enthusiasm, hurriedly raising their hands. Given the job involved a hose, it might just be fun.

Mr Mudge narrowed his eyes. 'Can I trust you lot?' he said.

'Yes, Mr Mudge,' they replied in unison.

'Mmm. Mo, you can go too.' Mr Mudge looked at Bella. 'Ms Ferosi, you too. You're in

charge. If any of these boys give you trouble, report them to me.'

'No problem, Mr Mudge.' Bella flicked her ponytail so hard it hit Davey in the eye.

Soon they were armed with gloves, garden forks and a bucket and heading for the petunia garden, Bella leading the way.

'Be careful to pull out only the weeds,' she instructed as she handed out the tools. 'The petunia plants have these big flowers on them and look like this.' She pointed. 'Now, let's get started.'

Davey reluctantly bent down and prised a weed out of the hard grey dirt. When he turned to throw it in the bucket, he saw that Bella was texting on her phone. 'Are you going to help?' he asked.

Bella gave her head a little shake, sending a shiver down her ponytail. 'I'm allergic to dirt,' she said.

Davey was already wishing he hadn't volunteered for this job. The weeding would take all lunchtime, leaving little time for the only fun bit – the watering. His friends looked as gloomy as he did.

Suddenly Mo began to work frantically. He gave Davey a push. 'Move over, Shorty. You're in my way,' he said. 'I'll get this job done in no time.'

The other boys stood back, amazed. Sure enough, Mo finished in minutes what would have taken them an hour.

'Very good, Mo,' Bella said. 'I'll tell Mr Mudge how you and I did most of the work.'

'Now the watering,' Mo said. He dusted off his hands and picked up the hose, which was connected to a tap around the corner. 'Here, Deep.' He handed the hose to Sunil. 'You hold this while I turn on the tap.'

Shrugging, Sunil took the hose. Never before had Mo been so diligent and helpful.

'Is it working?' Mo called from around the corner.

'No,' Sunil called back.

'What about now?' Mo had never sounded so friendly.

'Still not working.'

'Is it blocked?' Mo stuck his head around the corner. 'Maybe check the end.' His head disappeared.

Sunil couldn't resist. He held the hose up to his eye and looked into the end. A huge spray of water hit him in the face.

'Clouter! You're toast!' Still clutching the gushing hose, Sunil vanished around the corner.

Davey heard the two boys shouting. Bella looked shocked. Seconds later, Mo and Sunil reappeared, both soaked.

'That's it!' Bella stamped her foot. 'Wait till Mr Mudge hears about this!' She stormed off in search of the teacher.

By the time Mr Mudge arrived, all five boys were dripping wet.

'My petunias!' Mrs Trundle had appeared in the doorway of her office. 'Mr Mudge, what on earth is going on?' Mrs Trundle sounded as if she thought Mr Mudge was to blame, and her eye was twitching.

Mr Mudge's ears glowed scarlet. 'Mrs Trundle, I must apologise. I'd hoped to surprise you. Instead, these boys have behaved disgracefully.'

Davey noticed that Mudge's ears had now turned indigo and he was shaking. He looked like he might self-destruct at any moment. 'You five are on morning detention as well,' Mudge said, grinning malevolently. 'There'll be no time for ball games. None at all.'

Davey's heart sank. Now his secret weapon was surely dead in the water.

CHAPTER 8

DETENTION CIRCUMVENTION

There was no way Max would be allowed to attend morning detention, so Davey locked the dog inside before grabbing his bag and helmet and pushing his bike down the side path.

As usual, he'd packed Kaboom, but now that he was on detention both morning *and*

lunch, there'd be no time to play cricket and no time to practise his tricky switch hit at school. With only four days until the big game against the Crabby Creek Crickets, Davey had almost run out of time to get it right.

Out in the street, Sunil was loitering. He had one foot on his scooter but seemed reluctant to leave.

Davey climbed onto his bike, but he didn't feel like going either. 'I can't believe we have to spend every *morning* before school doing more stupid jobs with Smudge,' he groaned. 'And now Mum's got me sitting around with all the old fogeys at Uncle Vernon's every afternoon. 'When do we get to play cricket? It's so unfair!'

Sunil was usually the man with the plan, but today he seemed defeated. 'Yeah, it sure does suck,' he grumbled. 'And then to have to

spend all day and all lunchtime with Smudge.
It's intolerable!'

Sunil never used words like 'intolerable'.
He was clearly upset.

'It'll be worse than *intolerable* if we're late,'
Davey said. 'We'd better go.'

When the boys reported to the quadrangle
for morning detention, Kevin and George
were already there. Mo was there too,
kicking a football *at* them rather than *to*
them. Mr Mudge, however, was nowhere
to be seen.

Then the new teacher, Ms Maro, appeared
around the corner. She was leading a group of
Year Sixes from another class.

'Ah, here they are,' she said kindly.
'Mr Mudge is training the new lawn bowls
team this morning, so I offered to keep an eye
on you.' She smiled and Davey noticed what
nice brown eyes she had. 'Now, why don't you
boys give us a hand? We're getting ready for the
Welcome to Kindy showcase. There's lots to do!'

'Yes, Miss,' they mumbled. Helping Ms
Maro had to be better than polishing the
lawn bowls set, which is what Mudge had
threatened to make them do.

'Follow me!' the teacher exclaimed, as if
they were about to embark on an Easter egg
hunt in a magical forest. She led them to
A playground, where a group of gymnasts
wearing what looked like bandicoot ears were
practising on a vaulting horse.

The school choir was also gathered and
already halfway through the school song.

Lead soprano Bella Ferosi was front and centre.

Still another group of students were on the grass, painting signs that said things such as 'Kanga's Kakestall' and 'Possum's Potions'.

'Possum's Potions?' Davey whispered to his friends. They all looked at each other and shrugged.

Ms Maro thought for a moment. 'Now, boys, perhaps you'd like to stand at the back of the choir,' she said brightly. 'I'm sure you know the school song. If you're not confident to sing along, just mouth the words. You know, like they do in music videos.'

Mo grumbled but did what he was told, pushing his way past Bella and into the choir's back row.

Sunil looked at Davey, then George and Kevin. 'Actually, Miss, I've been meaning to talk to you.' He smiled so his dimple showed. 'We're in the school cricket team.' He nodded in the direction of his friends. 'And I thought we could give the kindy kids and their parents a demonstration. Get the kids interested in sport early, you know? Develop some new talent.'

Ms Maro looked at Sunil as if he were her long-lost son. 'That's a wonderful idea!' she said. 'Do you think the other team members might also join in? It'd be great to have you all there showcasing your skills!'

'I'm the captain, so I should be able to make it happen,' Sunil said in an authoritative voice. 'But if it's okay with you, we'll start practising now. Tomorrow I'll make sure the whole team's here. We've got our own gear with us, see?' He held up his cricket ball with one hand

and pointed to Kaboom, which was sticking out of Davey's bag, with the other.

'Excellent, Sunil. Mr Mudge will be thrilled to hear that you boys have offered to participate!'

Ms Maro really did have nice eyes, Davey noticed. Her smile was lovely too.

'It's probably safer if we take it down to B playground,' Sunil said helpfully.

'Certainly,' Ms Maro said. 'Off you go!'

Davey had to hand it to his friend – he *was* a genius!

The boys set off, trying not to cheer until they were well out of earshot.

'Boys!' Ms Maro was beckoning them back.

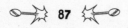

'I forgot to mention,' she said, when they stood before her once more. 'The theme for Welcome to Kindy this year is "Australian Animals".' She drew quotation marks in the air. 'So everyone will be dressed as marsupials.'

Ms Maro beamed as if she'd never heard of anything more fun. 'Why don't you dress up as kangaroos? The kindy kids will love it!'

'But where would we get the costumes from, Ms Maro?' There was an odd quaver in Sunil's voice that Davey rarely heard.

'You can help make them! All you need are ears and tails. We'll do the makeup on the day.'

'PPPPFFFfffffffffff! Ha-ha!' Mo Clouter, who had been standing in the back row of the choir scowling, was grinning like a demented pufferfish.

Ms Maro flashed Mo a warm smile. 'I know! It's going to be so much fun! Wait till you singers get *your* costumes!'

Mo's grin became a grimace.

CHAPTER 9

SECRET WEAPONS

With Ms Maro's blessing, Davey Warner and his friends managed to play some cricket during Monday's morning detention.

Sunil even convinced Ms Maro to speak to Mr Mudge about allowing them to practise for the Welcome to Kindy showcase during

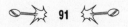

lunchtime detention. The boys didn't expect the new teacher to have any luck on that score, but when she visited the cricketers on Tuesday morning, she informed them that Mr Mudge had agreed.

'I wonder what she said to convince Smudge,' Davey whispered, as Ms Maro headed back to the relative safety of A playground.

'I dunno,' Sunil replied. 'But I'm starting to think she's tougher than she looks. Remember how she stood up to Mrs Trundle in assembly? I reckon she has some kind of secret weapon of her own.'

'She must have. She's got us dressing up as kangaroos . . .'

Detention was suddenly a whole lot more fun. With the whole team playing, it felt almost like a real match. Sunil, being captain, even went so far as to give Davey extra time at the crease, pounding him down the leg side so he could practise his switch hit, and letting him stay in even when he got out.

When the rest of the team complained about Davey getting all the batting time, Sunil bought them off with Whopper Chomps that he'd obtained on credit from Benny's shop.

It was an act of extreme generosity. 'Don't worry, Warner,' Sunil said when Davey fell over in shock. 'You'll have to pay Benny back – with interest. But first things first. You've gotta get this switch hit right before Saturday.'

Even Mr Mudge had a spring in his step. Like the cricketers, his new lawn bowls team were practising hard for the Welcome to Kindy showcase and were apparently showing great promise. Mr Mudge seemed more willing to overlook the minor misdemeanours of certain members of 6M. He even let slip that he'd agreed to dress up as a marsupial for the kindy welcome.

Only Mo, having been dragooned into the choir, seemed unhappy with the new arrangements. He was constantly whispering insults at Davey, and tried more than once to get him in trouble. But Davey didn't care. He wasn't the one having to practise lip syncing in the choir every morning.

By training on Tuesday evening, Davey's secret weapon was starting to come together. He was finding that he was better able to judge which balls to use it on, and his timing was improving, too. But when Benny finally arrived and gathered the team around him for his pre-training pep talk, he was decidedly unenthusiastic.

'We were lucky on Saturday and we probably didn't deserve it. And while I don't want to point the finger'—he pointed at Davey—'if we'd all taken our time and not tried anything clever, we could have done a lot better.' He looked Davey in the eye. 'You've got real talent, my friend. Don't waste it by taking silly risks. Ditch the switch, okay?'

Davey looked around at Sunil and George. Sunil's face showed no emotion, but he gave Davey a half-wink. George scratched his nose, but Davey noticed his friend had his fingers crossed.

'Now, I need to pop away for a short while to see—'

'—a man about a dog,' the Sluggers said as one.

Benny looked taken aback. 'Yeah, that's right. So get to it. I'll be back to pick up the gear.' He glanced again at Davey. 'Remember what I said . . .'

Davey nodded, but he'd already made up his mind. Ricky said he should go for it. His mum said he should go for it. Even his big brother, Steve, who never showed any interest in the Sluggers' fortunes, had said at breakfast that it could work. And, most importantly, *Davey* wanted to give it his best shot.

As soon as Benny's car turned the corner, the boys went back to their game. Sunil was in, but when Max caught him out (again), they started at the top of the batting order. Now Davey and George were in.

Dylan, their wicketkeeper, had a turn at bowling spin.

'Give Warner some down the leg side. And see if you can trick him with a googly,' Sunil called out.

Dylan bowled a few topspinners before surprising Davey with a flipper. Then he sent one down the leg side. Davey picked it, made the switch, hit it high and ran for three.

When he was back at the striker's end, Davey tried his switch again. It worked like a dream, and he slammed it high for four.

'You're getting better and better, Warner!' George called out.

'Yeah, good one!' Sunil called, running over. 'A bit more practice and it'll be a sure-fire scare-'em-off-the-pitch secret weapon.' He slapped Davey on the back. 'Along with my secret weapon, those Crickets won't have a hope!'

'Your secret weapon?' Davey frowned. 'Don't you go breaking any rules, Deep. We don't want to be disqualified.'

Sunil's expression was stern. 'I'd never do anything on the field that wasn't within the laws of cricket,' he said in his captain's voice.

At that moment, Ivy lobbed the ball in their direction. Davey caught it. 'Here. Stick to this secret weapon,' he said, handing the ball to Sunil. 'Now, give me one down the leg side.' He went back to his place at the crease.

Sunil bowled a bouncer. This time Davey's switch hit was perfect, and the ball went flying into the swamp.

'Six!' George shouted.

Max took off at a gallop. Moments later, he dropped the ball at Davey's feet.

'Thanks, boy,' Davey said, giving the dripping dog a pat. 'Aww, Max, now you stink again!'

CHAPTER 10

COSTUME CRICKET

By morning detention on Thursday, the
school cricket team's demonstration routine
for the Welcome to Kindy showcase was
coming together. Davey's switch hit was
looking even better. In fact, the team were
having so much fun they didn't want detention
to end.

When Davey and his friends did make it
to class, Mr Mudge was so preoccupied with
his lawn bowls team he not only failed to
notice they were late, but forgot to mark their
homework. It was a bonus for Davey and
Sunil, who'd forgotten to do it.

When at last it was lunchtime, they were
all itching to get to detention. On their way to
C playground, they spotted the school choir
practising.

Mo Clouter could be seen but not heard,
standing in the back row glaring.

Sunil give him a friendly wave.

Mo's face turned purple.

Ms Maro, who was sitting with a group
of kids on mats working with scissors and
glue, called the cricketers over. 'Tomorrow

morning we make the costumes, guys!' she cried, as though they'd just won a prize in a lucky dip. 'So come here as soon as you get to school. Then we've got the dress rehearsal at lunchtime.' Her brown eyes widened. 'I can't wait to see you all dressed up!'

'Ha ha!' Mo's face was wearing that awful pufferfish grin again.

Ms Maro nodded encouragingly at Mo.

'Can't you get us out of wearing ears and tails?' Davey hissed to Sunil once they were out of earshot. It was the only thing taking the shine off proceedings.

'I'm working on it. Maybe . . .'

Davey rounded the toilet block and spotted Max sitting patiently under a tree, waiting for the game to start.

'Oh-oh. Where's Smudge?' Davey said.

'With the lawn bowls team in B playground,' Kevin said. 'He'll be busy all lunchtime.'

'Good. Let's get started.'

When it was Davey's turn to bat, Max took up his position at silly mid-off and barked impatiently.

Kevin bowled a topspinner. Max stood ready to catch him again, but Davey switched sides and hit the ball to the boundary.

'Tricked you, brainless bow-wow!'

Max gave him the evil eye and trotted over to silly mid-on. He barked again.

Davey called out to Kevin. 'Give me another one like that!'

Kevin mixed it up, bowling a flipper.

Davey switched and slammed it high over Max's head.

'Max, you might as well go home,' Davey said. 'You're outclassed.'

Max sat on his haunches. *I'm not going anywhere*, he seemed to say. But when the bell rang, he made a dash for the gate and freedom.

Davey and his friends would have preferred to spend their second-last detention playing cricket, but as it turned out, making koala and kangaroo ears and tails wasn't as tedious as they'd expected.

The boys had to admit that Ms Maro's enthusiasm was contagious. She was so excited by all the fun to be had that soon they were laughing and joking as they glued pieces of fake fur onto cardboard and sewed long strips to elastic. It was certainly better than writing lines or picking up papers with Mr Mudge.

But dressing up in ears and tails was another matter, and when it was time for lunchtime detention on Friday they dawdled to A playground, where the dress rehearsal was to take place.

When they arrived, the school choir, now dressed as echidnas, were setting up. Mo looked like he'd eaten a bad prawn as he clambered into the back row.

Sunil and Davey gave him a friendly wave.

While the choir sang, the cricket team put on their costumes.

'You look like a meerkat,' Davey said to Sunil.

'And you look like an orangutan,' Sunil replied.

When the singing was over, Ms Maro clapped loudly. 'Beautiful!' she cried.

Next up were the bandicoot-eared gymnasts, who leapt and dived over the vaulting horse while the lawn bowls team, wearing platypus tails, set up. Directing proceedings were Mr Mudge and Mrs Trundle, but Davey was disappointed to see that neither teacher wore a tail.

The cricket team set up their wickets while the lawn bowlers ran through their routine. To Davey, lawn bowls seemed slow, even dull, but Mr Mudge and Mrs Trundle appeared to adore it, cheering and clapping and ooing and ahing. Davey couldn't understand it.

'Okay, guys, hit it!' Ms Maro shouted when at last it was the cricket team's turn.

Five minutes later, the cricket display was over and Ms Maro was brimming with admiration. 'You'll be playing for Australia one day!' she exclaimed, as everyone gathered around.

Sunil smiled so his dimple showed. 'Thanks, Ms Maro. But we'd play much better without the tails and ears. I'm worried we'll trip over or something.'

Davey, who was standing at Sunil's side, nodded. 'It could be dangerous, Miss,' he said.

'Yeah, it could be,' someone said in his ear.

Davey turned. Mo Clouter was standing right behind them. He had a look of concern on his face – for Ms Maro's benefit, Davey presumed.

Ms Maro was thoughtful for a moment. 'Mmm. We better trim a few centimetres off those tails, then.' She put her hand into her pocket and pulled out a hairpin. 'And we'll use these to make sure your headbands don't slip.'

As one, the cricket team sucked in a breath.

'Davey Warner, there's a packet of hairpins in my desk drawer. Run and get them while we start on the tails.'

Ms Maro looked so pleased with her solution to the problem that Davey didn't have the heart to argue. So he set off in the direction of the teacher's room. But after just one step he toppled like a skittle and landed heavily on the grass with Sunil on top of him.

Davey felt an excruciating pain in his right ankle. 'Owww! What did you do, Deep? Get off!' He gave his friend a push.

'I didn't do anything!' Sunil tried to scramble to his feet, but fell over again.

Davey glanced down. His kangaroo tail was tied in a neat bow with Sunil's.

Ms Maro had a quizzical look on her face. 'Are you boys all right?' she said.

Sunil sat up and untied the tails. Then he got to his feet and tried to pull Davey up.

'Owwww!' Davey yelled again. When he did manage to get back on his feet, he found he could only stand on his left leg. And where his right ankle had once been there was a red lump the size of a cricket ball bulging out of his grey sock.

'PPPppffffffffff!' Mo Clouter could no longer contain his amusement.

CHAPTER 11

MATCH UNFIT

Saturday dawned clear, sunny and still –
perfect weather for the big match between
the Sandhill Sluggers and the Crabby Creek
Crickets. Davey Warner's eyes snapped open
and locked with Ricky Ponting's. *Good luck,
mate*, Ricky seemed to say. *You can do it.*

Out in the kitchen, Davey's dad had rustled up scrambled eggs and toast with fresh orange juice. While Davey gobbled up his breakfast, his mum packed Kaboom, his helmet, his lucky waterbottle and some green zinc cream in a backpack and left it by the door.

'Ready?' she asked, as Davey shovelled the last forkful of egg into his mouth.

Davey nodded.

'Here you go, then.' She handed him his crutches.

Davey stood slowly and balanced on his right foot. Once he had a crutch under each arm, he made his way out to the car. Even though the match was on at Flatter Park, a few minutes' walk away, Davey would need a ride.

Sunil was waiting by the car door. 'Thought I might as well get a lift,' he said. 'Dad's bringing Lata down later.' He looked Davey up and down. 'You sure you need crutches? Maybe that doctor's wrong.'

'Mum's insisting.' Davey tried putting weight on his right foot. 'Owww! I can still bat, but you'll have to run for me.'

Sunil helped him into the car. 'Reckon you can still do your secret weapon?' He looked worried.

'Dunno,' Davey said, as Sunil loaded the crutches in through the car door. 'I need to be able to move my feet fast for that.'

When Benny saw Davey shambling across Flatter Park, he grimaced. 'Gosh, mate, that looks nasty. Guess you'll have to sit this match out, eh?'

Davey shook his head. 'Nup, I'm fine to bat. Just need Sunil to run for me.'

'You sure?' Benny looked from Davey to Sunil, clearly pessimistic.

'Fine by me,' Sunil said. 'Warner's going to be hitting all sixes and fours, so I won't have much to do.' He slapped Davey on the back so hard he almost fell off his crutches.

Benny narrowed his eyes. 'Well, no funny stuff, Davey.'

'Yes, boss.'

'I'm thinking you won't be fielding, though, eh?'

Davey shook his head.

'Well, we've got no twelfth man today, so

we'll be one down out there.' Benny sighed. 'Looks like those Crickets'll be singing.'

'Don't worry, Warner,' Sunil said when Benny had left, off to grab a sandwich from his shop across the road. 'You've got your secret weapon, and I've got mine. Between us, we can *squash* these Crickets.'

Davey frowned. 'Deep, don't you put us in it.'

Sunil smiled. 'Just something to keep it interesting.' He looked towards the road. 'Ah, here she is now.'

'Who?'

'Lata. She's doing a little job for me.'

'Lata? She's four!'

'Exactly. No one will suspect her.'

Davey shook his head. Sometimes it was better not to know. Sunil was clever, that's for sure, but his schemes didn't always pan out. Davey was about to say so when the umpire called the Sluggers' captain away for the toss of the coin.

The Crickets won the toss and elected to bat, so the Sluggers made their way out onto the field. Only Davey stayed behind, sitting by himself under a tree in a fold-up chair with his crutches beside him, stripes of green zinc cream on his nose.

The match started slowly. George was bowling, but the Crickets weren't taking any chances, hitting ones and twos and offering up no catches.

Davey watched, his fingers and toes crossed that a batter would get bored and do something risky. He glanced over at Lata.

She was a short distance away, watching the game with Sunil's dad and all the other Sluggers' supporters. When she saw Davey look over, she gave him a big wave.

'Hi!' Davey called. He'd need to keep an eye on her, he decided.

Then he noticed that one of the Crickets' supporters, who were sitting under trees further off, was waving in his direction, shouting. 'Hey, Shorty!' It was Mo with that pufferfish grin.

What's he doing here? Davey wondered. Mo hated cricket.

Out on the field, the Crickets were warming up and off to a solid start.

Davey glanced over at Lata again. Now she was near the Crickets' camp, throwing a stick for Max. She saw Davey look over and waved

again. She held up the packet of what looked like TizzyFizz sherbet. 'Yum!'

Davey gave her the thumbs up.

'Out!'

Sunil had clean-bowled one of the Crickets' opening batters for thirteen runs. Davey and the Sluggers' supporters clapped. Lata cheered.

'Boo!' It was Mo.

The Crickets' number-three batter made his way out to the pitch. Davey glanced over at Lata. Now she'd found a tennis ball and was throwing it to Max, who was catching it on the full. It looked harmless enough.

Sunil quickly took another wicket. Two overs later he trapped the Crickets' number four LBW with an inswinger.

Suddenly there was a bark. Max was chasing Lata's tennis ball across the field. Then he spotted some seagulls and tore off after them. The birds rose as one. Max began dashing around in circles, snapping at the air.

'Max! Get back here!' Davey shouted, grabbing his crutches and scrambling to his feet.

Max ignored him.

Davey didn't go after him – he knew it would be pointless trying to round up the dog on crutches.

The umpire called a halt to proceedings while supporters from both sides tried to herd the dog back to the boundary. But Max was having none of it, and it took them ten minutes to catch him and tether him to the fence so the match could continue.

Davey sat down again. *Was that Deep's secret weapon?* he wondered. If it was, it didn't work. In fact, the disturbance seemed to focus the Crickets. As if they suddenly had Sunil's number, they began hitting him around the park. Several fours and a couple of sixes later, they'd lost no more wickets and were racking up runs fast.

Even when George took over the bowling, the Crickets kept up the pressure. By morning tea and the end of the innings, they'd lost no more wickets and had scored ninety-two runs. It was a strong effort and Davey knew it'd be hard to beat.

The Sluggers looked red-faced and disappointed as they came off the field.

Back from the shop, Benny was handing out the water bottles. 'Not a bad effort, guys,' he said, 'but there's no doubt those Crickets are on top.' He offered around the cut-up oranges. 'You've got an uphill battle. With Davey here on crutches, I'd say it's looking almost impossible.'

Sunil let out a groan.

'I know how you feel, mate,' Benny said.

Sunil growled and shook his head.

Davey had never seen his friend so miserable after an innings.

'Yeah, it's terrible,' Benny moaned, nodding.

'*Lata!* What have you *done*?' Sunil threw his piece of orange in the dirt and took off after his little sister.

Thinking it was a game, Lata ran away, giggling. Her dad watched, bemused.

Davey glanced at his teammates. Every single Slugger had a look of disgust on their face.

'Eeewww!' they yelled.

Now George threw his piece of orange in the dirt. 'These oranges are revolting!'

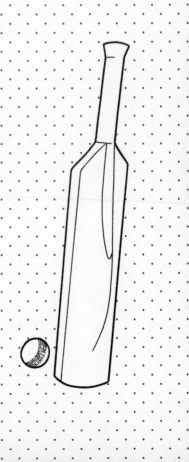

CHAPTER 12

BATTING FROM BEHIND

The Sluggers' oranges tasted so disgusting they had to be thrown in the bin.

'Any chance you could bring some over from the shop?' Davey's mum asked Benny.

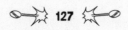

Benny shook his head. 'None there. Barb threw them out yesterday. They'd gone all green and powdery.'

In the end, the Crickets gave the Sluggers their leftovers, but there wasn't enough to go round and most Sluggers went without.

Around the other side of the field, Sunil was speaking sternly to his little sister. No one could hear what he was saying, but when he'd finished, Lata marched back to her father with a furious frown on her face. Sunil looked just as irate as he returned to the sideline to pad up.

'What was all that about?' Davey asked his friend as they pulled on their helmets.

'Tell you later,' Sunil mumbled. 'Suffice to say my secret weapon's no longer operational. We're counting on yours now, Warner.'

Davey grimaced inside his helmet. Now he had a sprained ankle, he doubted whether he'd be able to pull off his switch hit. It took some fancy footwork, but he could barely stand on two feet, let alone make them dance.

When the batters and the runner were ready, they made their way out to the wicket, Sunil and George half-carrying Davey as he hopped across the grass. 'Owww!' he yelped more than once.

In contrast to the hot, tired and hungry Sluggers, the Crickets looked fresh-faced as they took their positions. Calum, their captain, set a tight attacking field, so much so the umpire had to order some of his players to take a step back from the pitch.

Davey and Sunil stood at the bowler's end and waited. George took his position at the crease.

The Sluggers got off to a slow start, thanks to a strong opening spell from one of the Crickets' best bowlers. Her first ball was wide, but from then on her line was good and the length varied enough to keep George on his toes.

George let the first few go through. It wasn't until the last ball of the over that he pulled off a glance past fine leg. He and Sunil ran for three.

During the next two overs, George played well, taking his time but making the most of any opportunities. Then, after George made a graceful sweep to square leg, Davey found himself at the crease.

Davey's plan was to take his time and try to play as much as possible off his good back foot. He left as many balls as he played, blocking singles when the ball was full, before playing a pull and hook through the leg side. He'd decided to use his switch hit only as a last resort because the footwork was so tricky, especially with a cricket ball for an ankle.

But the Crickets were on to him, and soon the bowler was sending down full-length balls to try to tempt Davey onto his injured front foot. Davey resisted the bait, sticking with his defensive shots and the odd back-foot drive when he could. But his aching ankle told him that his secret weapon, which depended on turning on his front foot, was probably a no-go.

In the fifteenth over, the Sluggers suffered a hammer blow when George tried a cut shot and was caught behind for thirty-one. Davey watched as his friend trudged back to the bench. The Sluggers were now on fifty-two. They'd need to pick up their run rate to get close to the Crickets.

Number three in the Sluggers' order was Ivy. As soon as she came to the crease, she was looking good. Davey watched as she hit a four off her second ball, before driving to deep extra cover for three more.

As Davey waited for the next ball, he looked across at Sunil.

'You okay?' his friend asked.

'Yeah, but I can't move my right foot so well.'

The bowler delivered an inswinger. Davey drove it to long-on. Sunil and Ivy ran, and ran again. The long-on fielder fumbled the ball, so they tried for another run. Suddenly the ball was in the hands of the bowler, who threw it at the wicket. As Sunil dived into the crease, the bails flew.

The Crickets leapt into the air. 'Out!'

Sunil clambered to his feet but stood his ground. Davey looked at the umpire, his heart in his mouth.

The umpire didn't move.

'That was out!' someone yelled from the sideline. It was Mo. He was still standing with the Crickets' supporters, waving his arms like an unhinged octopus.

The umpire still didn't move. 'Not out,' he said finally.

The Crickets shook their heads and went back to their positions. But even from the other end, Davey could see that his friend *had* made it in time.

As Sunil took up his position as runner at the bowler's end, he turned and gave Mo a friendly wave.

'Go the Crickets!' Mo hollered. Davey could see that even the Crickets' supporters were looking sideways at the bellowing turnip.

But while Davey had lived to see another over, Ivy was out LBW two overs later. After that, the Sluggers' middle order wavered, losing their next six wickets for just eighteen runs.

At eight wickets down for eighty-three, Sunil was batting next, so George came back out to run for Davey.

As the Sluggers' captain made his way to the striker's end, Davey took a deep breath. If he didn't pick up the pace, victory would soon be out of the Sluggers' reach and they'd lose their number-two position on the ladder. Davey knew he probably shouldn't have cared too much, but he did – a lot.

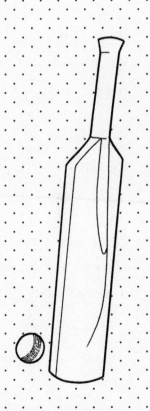

CHAPTER 13

SWITCH OR NIX

The Crickets' best paceman let the ball
fly. The ball looked straight and Sunil
played at it. But at the last moment it
swung out, glancing off the bat's edge and
sailing straight into the keeper's waiting
hands.

Sunil was out – for a golden duck. Shaking his head, his face set in a grimace, he walked.

The umpire raised his arm and the Crickets and their supporters cheered.

'YEAH!' someone thundered. It was Mo.

Davey watched as Joe, the Sluggers' last batter, trudged across the field to the striker's crease. With only two overs to go, the Sluggers needed ten runs to win. That meant at least five runs each over, which was much more than their current run rate.

Two balls went through before Joe played a late cut to backward point for one. Now Davey was at the crease, and the Crickets quickly changed their field for the left-hander.

Again the bowler tried to draw Davey onto his front foot, forcing him to let the ball go

through to the keeper. On the last ball of
the over, he managed to pull off a back-foot
cover drive. George and Joe ran a single. The
fielder fumbled the ball, so they ran again and
managed to turn the single into a three.

With one over left, the Sluggers were now
five behind and Davey was at the striker's
end again.

But halfway through the final over,
Kaboom hadn't even smelt leather let alone
struck it. When the fourth ball came down the
leg side, Davey decided it was now or never,
and turned, swapped his hands and made to
drive it up and over. Instead, the ball nicked
the edge and was just short of being caught
in slips.

There were two balls to go and the Sluggers
were still five runs behind.

'CRACK 'EM, YOU CRABBY CREEK CRICKETS!' Mo's face looked like it might pop at any moment.

Davey breathed in, wiggled his shoulders and took his position again. 'Come on, we can do it,' he whispered, tapping Kaboom on the pitch in front of him. But he had to let the bouncer go through. Now there was only one ball left.

The bowler sent it down the leg side, perhaps hoping that Davey would make the same mistake as last time. On this occasion, however, Davey turned on his foot and switched his hands as if he'd been doing it since he was born. He swung Kaboom and hooked the ball high into the air. It flew towards the boundary and over.

'Six! SIX!' This time Kaboom didn't leap out of his hands and make a bow, nor did the

fielders transmogrify into seagulls. This
time, it was for real. Davey Warner had done
a switch hit for six.

The Sluggers had won.

'No-o-o-o-o-o!' It was Mo. Now he *did* look
like a pufferfish.

That afternoon, Sunil and Davey were lying
on the grass in the backyard sucking
on Whopper Chomps and discussing the
morning's events.

'I lined up Lata to put bi-carb soda on their
oranges,' Sunil admitted. 'I was hoping it
might react with the acid in the oranges and
make them froth. Thought that might freak
out the Crickets and put them off their game.
But it just made their oranges taste weird.'

'*Our* oranges, you mean. She did it to *our* oranges.' Davey gave his friend a kick with his good leg.

'Mmm, that's what I thought too.' Sunil looked a little remorseful. 'Actually, Lata did put it on *their* oranges, while everyone was chasing Max around the field. But Mo saw her do it and as soon as she walked away, he switched them with ours.'

'How do you know?'

'He couldn't wait to tell me, as soon as I got out. He also told me how much he enjoyed seeing me go down for a golden duck.'

'Yeah, I guess he would have liked that.'

Sunil grinned. 'That's okay. I'll get him back another day. And anyway, thanks to your secret weapon, we won, which Mo must have hated even more. Ha!'

'Sunil! Are you ready?' Lata was peering over the top of the fence.

'Okay.' He sat up and dusted himself off. 'I've got to go. Things to do.'

'You're not cooking up more secret weapons, I hope,' Davey said.

'Nah, I promised to teach Lata her times tables. She already knows some of them,' Sunil said proudly.

'Lucky Lata,' Davey said. 'After all, you're such an *expert*.'

'True.' Sunil stood and stretched, then headed down the side path. 'Watch out!' he called. 'Here comes Max the Axe!'

Davey heard a bark. Max appeared. Zipping across the grass, the dog jumped on Davey and licked his face.

'Get off!' Davey gave the dog a push. 'Aaarrgghh! What have you been rolling in? You stink!'

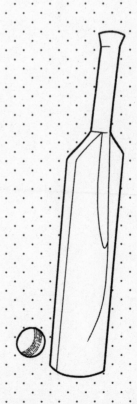

CHAPTER 14

WELCOME TO KINDY CRICKET SPECTACULAR

In the end, the Welcome to Kindy showcase turned out better than Davey and his friends expected. Even though they felt silly in marsupial makeup and headbands with ears, and despite the fact that everyone said they looked more like bush rats than kangaroos, it was fun to be something other than eleven-year-old boys for a few hours.

Davey had to admit that nice Ms Maro had done a good job. There were stalls selling cakes and drinks and funny signs telling people where to go and what to do. She'd even managed to convince the teachers to dress up as Australian animals, which seemed to put them in a better mood.

When Mr Mudge appeared in a giant sugar glider costume, Davey nearly fell off his crutches. The usually grumpy teacher was only surpassed by Mrs Trundle, who looked almost approachable as a ringtail possum.

Davey did feel a bit sorry for the kindy kids, who probably thought that school was going to be like this every day from here on. *Just you wait*, he thought.

Sunil and Davey were loitering by the cake stall when Ms Maro bustled over in her quokka costume. 'Come on, boys. Time to set up for the cricket display. Davey, will you be okay on those crutches?'

Davey nodded. 'They're just for show now, Miss. And to keep Mum happy.'

'Well, that's the most important thing.' She flashed him a big smile. She really did have the loveliest eyes, Davey thought.

While Ms Maro and some Year Six quolls directed people to their seats, the cricketers set up and took their positions. At the same time, the choir of echidnas filed onto the temporary stage.

Ms Maro spoke a few words of welcome, then Bella grabbed the microphone. 'I'm Bella Ferosi, school captain and the choir's lead soprano,' she said, giving her echidna spines a flick. 'Today we're singing the school song. It's called "Give Your Best – If Possible", after the school motto.'

Sunil gave a friendly wave in the direction of the choir. 'Check out Clouter,' he whispered.

Davey glanced over. Mo stood in the middle of the back row, his shoulders slumped and teeth bared. His furry ears were lopsided and his nose had smudged. He looked like the most miserable echidna ever born.

The choir burst into song, but Davey could tell even from a distance that Mo wasn't singing. For one thing, his mouth didn't move once.

When the singing was over and the applause had died down, it was time for the bandicoot gymnasts. Once the last vault had been executed, the lawn bowls team trooped onto the grass beside the stage.

As the team played a mock tournament, Mr Mudge gave a commentary.

Once again, Davey thought how slow and dull the game seemed, but the kids were genuinely enjoying it. As for Mr Mudge, well, his ears glowed a rosy peach as he described every move of the players and explained the rules.

'There's nothing like it,' he concluded. 'Skill, luck, strategy, action, excitement. It's all of these rolled into one glossy, beautiful bowling ball of a game.' Davey saw Mr Mudge glance at Mrs Trundle. 'Wouldn't you agree?'

Mrs Trundle's eye hadn't twitched all morning and it didn't start now. Instead, she smiled. 'Mr Mudge, you have taken the words right out of my mouth.'

At that moment, Ms Maro stepped forward. 'Thank you, Mr Mudge, Mrs Trundle. Now I have the pleasure of introducing the school cricket team. And what a team they are!' She looked across at the cricketers. 'Okay, guys, hit it!'

As planned, Sunil bowled to George, who hit it neatly to Kevin, who caught it on the bounce, and George ran for one. Sunil bowled an inswinger to Ivy, who hit it neatly to Talia at cover, who threw it to Kevin, who came in to bowl. Kevin's leg break went through, as intended, to Dylan, the keeper, who stumped George, at which point Davey tossed his crutches aside and ran to the crease with Kaboom. As previously agreed, Kevin bowled a flipper. Davey spun like a ballerina, swapped his hands and performed his amazing switch hit as if he were playing for Australia.

The ball sailed through the air like a heat-seeking missile. It grazed Mr Mudge's left ear, which spontaneously turned from peach to purple. But just as Mr Mudge was about to explode, the crowd cheered.

'Out!' It was Mo. He was standing by the cake stall and had managed to get his hands to the ball. But already he was toppling backwards. With a crash, he fell into the cakes and dropped the ball, sending cupcakes, muffins and toffees flying in every direction.

The kindy kids had been sitting quietly on the mats at the front watching the display. Now they jumped to their feet and ran laughing and shouting after the baked goods.

While the parents and teachers rounded up the kindies and cakes, Ms Maro helped the cricketers and bowlers put away their gear. 'That was a wonderful display,' she said to Sunil and Davey, as they packed the wickets and bails into carry cases.

'Thanks, Miss. Glad you enjoyed it,' Sunil said.

'You boys won't know what to do with yourselves, now you're finished with detention, will you?' There was sympathy in Ms Maro's voice.

Sunil smiled so his dimple showed. 'Guess not. What'll we do, Warner?'

'Not sure. Play lawn bowls, I guess.'

'Mr Mudge and Mrs Trundle certainly enjoy it,' Ms Maro said, her brown eyes sparkling. 'You might find you like it.'

Sunil shrugged. 'Maybe.'

'Hmmm.' Davey looked up at Ms Maro. 'You never know,' he said, smiling.

But he did know. Cricket was his game, and it always would be. For one thing, in lawn bowls they didn't use bats. What kind of game was that? And how could he possibly play a game without Kaboom?

It wasn't worth thinking about.

Did you enjoy *The Big Switch*?
Another adventure of The Kaboom Kid
is available now!

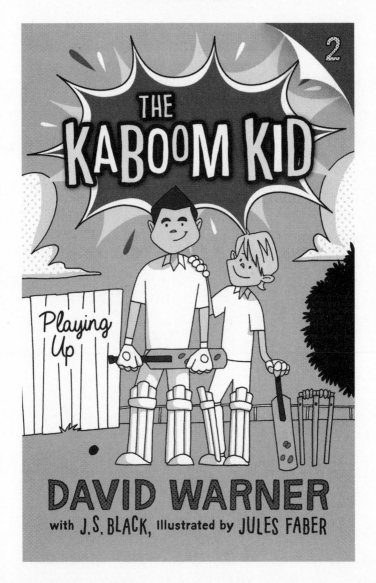

More fun with
The Kaboom Kid
coming soon!